This book is dedicated to my
daughter Vita, whom I love more than infinity.

And to my mom, Rose Joseph, who passed away last year. She
emerged from the Bergen Belsen Concentration Camp to raise
our family, and is the ultimate survivor!

www.mascotbooks.com

The Last Surviving Dinosaur: The TyrantoCrankaTsuris

For more information, please contact:
Mascot Books
620 Herndon Parkway, Suite 320
Herndon, VA 20170
info@mascotbooks.com

Library of Congress Control Number:2018909920

CPSIA Code: PRT0119A
ISBN-13: 978-1-64307-157-2

Printed in the United States

THE LAST
SURVIVING DINOSAUR

The TyrantoCrankaTsuris

Steven Joseph

Illustrated by Andy Case

"Tsuris" is the Yiddish word for problems. Now, when I say "problems," I'm not talking about minor daily inconveniences. I'm talking about major life-changing traumatic events that have brought on such suffering that has never been experienced by anyone since the beginning of time and something you would never wish on your worst enemy.

Consider the differences in these two statements: "I have this problem."

I grew up in a home in the Bronx. And like many other homes in my neighborhood, all my relatives loved to get together and start talking about their "tsuris."

"You think you have tsuris? If I had your tsuris, I'd be doing cartwheels! Nobody can outdo my tsuris!"

We all kvetched (which means "complaining about your tsuris") with a huge sense of pride. For us, it was as if we were training for the Tsuris Olympics. Only one of us could get the gold!

"How are you doing, Aunt Zaydie?"

"I am okay, but after the doctors got my warts off my feet, the nails came off with them!" My second cousin Dottie would chime in, "I'd be happy with no nails! I got my warts removed, but they were replaced by green fungus between my toes! I am talking about a forest growing on my feet!"

Aunt Ruthie leaned in and exclaimed, "Oy! But you both did not go through what I went through. I was in Florida and got bit by an alligator. And this is what I got! I am turning into a reptile!"

On the other side of the room, the men would talk.
"How are you doing, Uncle Mottie?"

"I could be better. For years, I thought I had this terrible dandruff problem. But nothing helped. Well, turns out it was lice. I am a walking plague!"

My cousin Whiny would interrupt: "Don't talk to me about lice. I got ticks! Deer ticks!! Only I can get deer ticks in Brooklyn!"

Uncle Shmukie, with his booming voice, always grabbed the gold. "I'd take lice and ticks in a heartbeat! I just got back from the doctor, and I have an inoperable brain tumor. The doctor says it's not life threatening, but they had to put a metal plate around it to keep it from growing. Now I can't fly on airplanes! They think I am carrying a bomb inside my head!"

All this tsuris training prepared me very well for when I became a father. The first time my daughter had a temper tantrum, I put her in time-out and told her that when she was done, I would tell her the real story about how all the dinosaurs but one went extinct.

When her time-out was over, she said, "I am ready for the story, Daddy! But you said that not all dinosaurs are extinct. That's not what I learned in school!"

"It's true, one little dinosaur survived. And even though she was the smallest dinosaur, she was the most dangerous of all. Believe it or not, we humans are all descendants from this one tiny dinosaur. She was called...the TyrantoCrankaTsuris!"

"The TyrantoCrankaTsuris was the smallest dinosaur on the planet, and all the other dinosaurs made fun of her because of her size."

"All the other dinosaurs liked to brag about how tough they were! 'I can eat an entire forest with one bite!!' one said."

"'My teeth are so big, they're the size of an entire forest!' a second exclaimed.

"'I floss my teeth with an entire forest!' boasted a third."

"And they laughed and laughed at the little TyrantoCrankaTsuris, until one day, the little TyrantoCrankaTsuris got really really mad and let out the biggest and loudest CrankaTsuris:

'I had bad warts on my toes but then they came off and my toenails came off with them, and then the fungus on my feet grew into the size of an entire forest, so I went to Florida to soak my feet in the ocean, and an alligator bit off the feet forest, but it bit my feet too and it hurts sooooo much!'"

"And with that CrankaTsuris, the whole planet shook and went dark."

"But the TyrantoCrankaTsuris would not stop: 'And I thought I had bad dandruff, but it was really lice, and then I found out that I had deer ticks even though deer don't even exist yet, and I can't get the deer ticks removed because I have a brain tumor, and if they tried to remove the deer ticks, my brains would splatter all over, and my head would hurt even worse!'"

"She went on and on and on, cranking out the tsuris until all the bigger, badder dinosaurs had vanished."

"Oh. There was one dinosaur that was immune to the CrankaTsuris. It was another tiny dinosaur, the TyrantoKvetchaTsuris!"

"And when the TyrantoKvetchaTsuris arrived from Florida with the alligator, they fell in love and lived crankily and kvetchily ever after!"

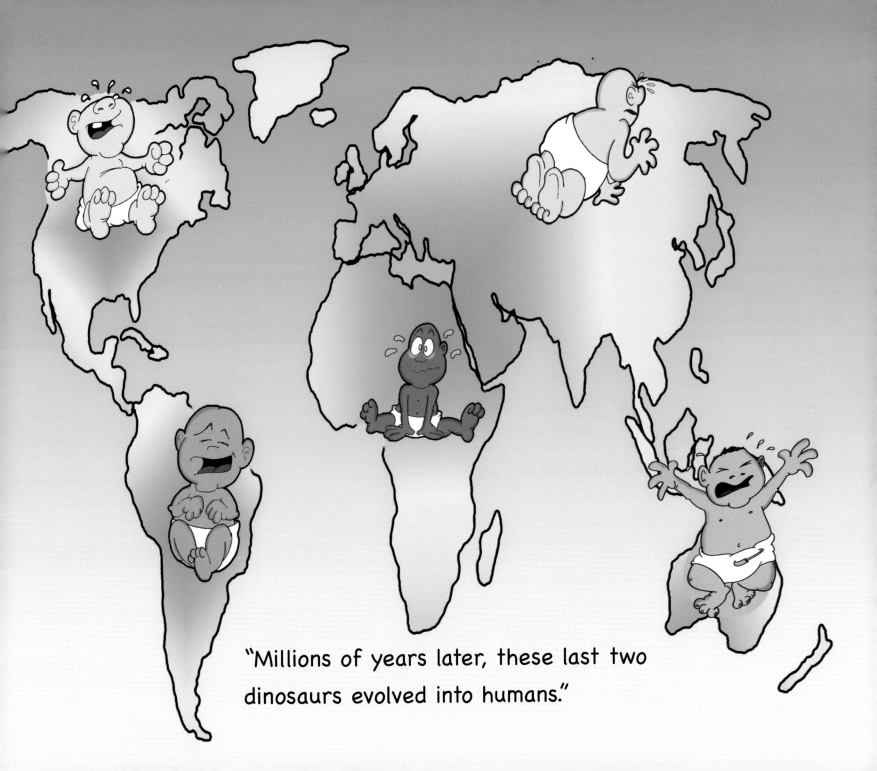

"Millions of years later, these last two dinosaurs evolved into humans."

"Before, you were getting a bit cranky and kvetchy. That's the part of us that we inherited from the TyrantoCrankaTsuris and the TyrantoKvetchaTsuris. Even Mommy and Daddy can be a CrankaTsuris and a KvetchaTsuris sometimes!"

"You need to be careful with this power," I told my daughter. "Remember, all the other dinosaurs went extinct because the TyrantoCrankaTsuris just wouldn't stop!"

So we learned to be careful not to express our inner TyrantoCrankaTsuris or TyrantoKvetchaTsuris too often. Just the right amount to keep the planet happy and not too cranky.

ABOUT THE AUTHOR

Steven Joseph was born in the Bronx, New York. He is a proud father of his beautiful grown-up daughter Vita and currently lives in Hoboken, New Jersey.